D1502522

PRESENTED TO:

Dad

FROM:

Randy & Judy

DATE:

Fathers Day 2001

Always Loved, Never Forgotten

ROY LESSIN

HB

HONOR
BOOKS

Always Loved, Never Forgotten
ISBN 1-56292-642-X
Copyright © 2001 by Roy Lessin
Published by Honor Books
P.O. Box 55388
Tulsa, Oklahoma 74155

Designed by Greg Jackson, Jackson Design Company,
Siloam Springs, Arkansas, jdesign@ipa.net

Illustrated by Todd Williams.

*T*here is never a time when He is
indifferent to our pain or unresponsive to our needs.
His arms are always open. His ear is always
listening. His eye is always watching.
His heart is always loving.

The need for us to encourage one another is the
aim of this book. I hope the thoughts and scriptures
in *From God's Heart to Yours* will help bring special
reminders of God's love and daily care for you.

~ ROY LESSIN ~

Bless the Lord, O my soul,
and forget not all his benefits.

PSALM 103:2

*T*here is never a time
you're not in His thoughts,
never a time without grace,
never a time when He turns away
from any need you face.

~

There is never a time
you're not in His heart,
never a time without love,
never a time when you're not blessed
with good things from above!

*How precious also are thy thoughts
unto me, O God! How great is the sum
of them! If I should count them, they
are more in number than the sand:
when I awake, I am still with thee.*

PSALM 139:17–18

*M*any things we face try to rob us of
the sense of God's peace and presence in
our lives. Pressures, hectic schedules,
difficulties, and disappointments are some
of the enemies that war against us.

~

Amid life's stress we need to be reminded
of the heart and mind of God toward us.
He assures us that we are never out of His
thoughts and always close to His heart.

The Lord hath appeared
of old unto me,
saying, Yea, I have loved thee
with an everlasting love:
therefore with lovingkindness
have I drawn thee.

JEREMIAH 31:3

Trust Me as your Heavenly Father.
I am the guardian and keeper of your soul.
I watch over you with an everlasting love.
I am conforming you to My image
and perfecting My love within you.
In Me is your identity, your confidence,
your courage, and your strength.
You bear My name, and
I delight in calling you My child.

For you have been my hope,
O Sovereign Lord, my
confidence since my youth.
From birth I have relied
on you; you brought me forth
from my mother's womb.

~

PSALM 71:5–6 NIV

His banner over
me was love.

~

SONG OF SOLOMON 2:4

*B*ecause I am faithful,
you can depend on Me.
Because I am wise,
you can turn to Me.
Because I am good,
you can walk with Me.
Because I am mighty,
you can lean on Me.
Because I am love,
you can trust in Me.

*Now we have received,
not the spirit of
the world, but the spirit
which is of God;
that we might know
the things that are
freely given to us of God.*

~

1 CORINTHIANS 2:12

God will never leave you empty.
If something is taken away,
He will replace it with something better.
If He denies your request in a certain area,
it is because He wishes to give you what is best.
If He asks you to put something down,
it is so you can pick up something greater.
God is not the great denier,
but the great giver.
He is not a robber,
but the bestower
of every good and perfect gift.

O Lord,
you have examined my heart
and know everything about me.
You know when I sit or stand.
When far away you know my every
thought.... Every moment, you know
where I am.... You both precede
and follow me, and place your
hand of blessing on my head.
This is too glorious,
too wonderful to believe!

~

PSALM 139:1–3, 5–6 TLB

*G*od is working
in more ways than you have asked Him.
He is doing more things
for you than your faith can imagine!

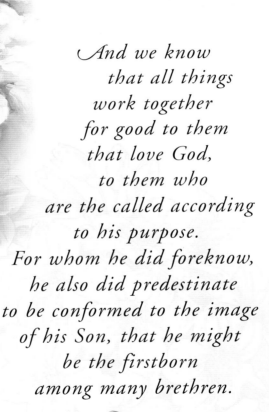

*And we know
    that all things
    work together
    for good to them
    that love God,
    to them who
    are the called according
    to his purpose.
    For whom he did foreknow,
    he also did predestinate
    to be conformed to the image
    of his Son, that he might
    be the firstborn
    among many brethren.*

ROMANS 8:28–29

I make all things beautiful.
Put your faith in Me,
not in a timetable.
Wait on Me and wait for Me.
When I am ready,
you will be ready.
In My perfect way,
I will put everything together,
see to every detail,
arrange every circumstance,
change every heart,
and order every step
to bring to pass
what I have for you.

*For I know the thoughts
that I think toward you,
saith the Lord, thoughts of
peace, and not of evil,
to give you an expected end.*

JEREMIAH 29:11

When we look back
and wonder how we ever
made it this far, we realize
it is not because we have been clever,
but because God has been wise;
not because we have been strong,
but because God has been mighty;
not because we have been consistent,
but because God has been faithful.

*For as the heavens are higher
than the earth, so are my ways
higher than your ways, and
my thoughts than your thoughts....
For ye shall go out with joy,
and be led forth with peace:
the mountains and the hills
shall break forth before you
into singing, and all the trees
of the field shall clap their hands.
Instead of the thorn
shall come up the fir tree,
and instead of the brier
shall come up the myrtle tree:
and it shall be to the Lord
for a name, for an everlasting sign
that shall not be cut off.*

ISAIAH 55:9,12–13

The mind of God is different
from the thoughts of man.
As we follow Him we discover
that we lose to gain,
surrender to win,
die to live,
give to receive,
serve to reign,
and scatter to reap.
In weakness we are made strong.
In humility we are lifted up.
In emptiness we are made full!

"If anyone is thirsty,
let him come to me and drink.
Whoever believes in me,
as the Scripture has said,
streams of living water will
flow from within him."

~

JOHN 7:37–38 NIV

Cast all your anxiety on him
because he cares for you.

~

I PETER 5:7 NIV

"Come to me, all you
who are weary and burdened,
and I will give you rest."

~

MATTHEW 11:28 NIV

We can give our tears to God
because He is our comforter,
our fears because He is our confidence,
our pains because He is our healer,
our stress because He is our peace, and
our heaviness because He is our joy!

*For the Lord thy God hath blessed
thee in all the works of thy hand:
he knoweth thy walking through this
great wilderness...the Lord thy God
hath been with thee;
thou hast lacked nothing.*

DEUTERONOMY 2:7

We don't walk alone;
we don't live abandoned.
Even in the wilderness
the streams of living water flow,
in the desert is a fount of blessing,
and in the dry place
are springs of everlasting joy.

ROY LESSIN

Never will I leave you;
never will I forsake you.

HEBREWS 13:5 NIV

A stranger may walk behind you,
but I am your friend and walk beside you.
A stranger may be unfamiliar with your ways,
but I am your friend and know your heart.
A stranger may not know how you feel,
but I am your friend and share your
joy and your pain. A stranger may keep
things from you, but I am your friend
and freely give you My love.

*For the Lord
seeth not as man seeth;
for man looketh
on the outward
appearance,
but the Lord
looketh on the heart.*

1 SAMUEL 16:7

I see the things
no one else can see.
I see your dreams
and all you long to be.
I see your faith—
I've seen it from the start.
I see the love
you carry in your heart.

Yet there is one ray of hope:
his compassion never ends.
It is only the Lord's mercies that
have kept us from complete destruction.
Great is his faithfulness; his
lovingkindness begins afresh each day.

LAMENTATIONS 3:21–23 TLB

God is not the kind of Father
Who tells us to pray
so He can turn us down,
to trust Him
so He can deny us,
or to receive His promises
so He can disappoint us.
Rather, He is compassionate and
tender to His faithful children.

*And what can David
say more unto thee?
for thou, Lord God,
knowest thy servant.*

2 SAMUEL 7:20

God is always ahead of you.

~

He loved you
before you gave your heart to Him.
He provided all things
before you had a need.
He knew all things
before you had a question.
He conquered all
before He asked you to overcome.
He gave Himself
before He asked you to touch others.
He prepares the way
before He asks you to follow.

"*For the Father himself loves you dearly, because you love me and believe that I came from the Father.*"

JOHN 16:27 TLB

When we asked for bread,
He didn't give us a stone;
When we sought His presence,
He didn't leave us alone;
When we needed a Savior,
He came from above;
When our hearts were empty,
He filled them with love.

*But as it is written,
eye hath not seen,
nor ear heard,
neither have entered
into the heart of man,
the things which God
hath prepared for them
that love him. But God
hath revealed them unto us
by his Spirit: for the Spirit
searcheth all things, yea,
the deep things of God.*

1 CORINTHIANS 2:9–10

To understand God's ways
we must see beyond the moment
to the end thing that He is doing.
We must never judge things prematurely.
What appears to be weakness,
God can transform into greatness.
What seems to be loss,
He can turn to gain.
What looks like failure,
He can turn to victory.
The hard thing you are going through
is not the final chapter.
There is more to be seen and known.
God's ways always bring about happy endings
to those who leave the final word with Him.

*But because of his
great love for us,
God, who is rich in mercy,
made us alive with Christ
even when we were dead in
transgressions—it is by grace
you have been saved.*

EPHESIANS 2:4-5 NIV

The difficulties in our lives
will pass on and we will move on.
We will move on in grace,
renewed in faith and
strengthened in character,
assured that God has
used the difficulty
to do His good work within us,
and to bring comfort
to others through us.

*Since, then, you have been raised
with Christ, set your hearts on things
above, where Christ is seated
at the right hand of God.
Set your minds on things above,
not on earthly things.
For you died, and your life
is now hidden with Christ in God.*

COLOSSIANS 3:1–3 NIV

God's ways are good;
they will be joy to you.
His ways are right;
they will be wisdom to you.
His ways are true;
they will be liberty to you.
His ways are pure;
they will be refreshment to you.
His ways are sure;
they will be strength to you.
His ways are best;
they will be blessings to you.

Behold, what manner of love the Father hath bestowed upon us, that we should be called the sons of God.

~

1 JOHN 3:1

You are God's child.
He likes listening to the sound of your voice.
Your heart and His are always in touch.
There are no laws or human barriers
that can keep you from your Father's presence:
no darkness that can hide His face,
no burden that can diminish His power,
no trial that can quench His love.

*For the eyes of the Lord
run to and fro
throughout the whole earth,
to shew himself strong
in the behalf of them
whose heart is perfect
toward him.*

2 CHRONICLES 16:9

Our courage in following Jesus is the assurance that we are moving in the right direction. What is right is not always popular. God wants us to walk as those who know they have chosen the higher way. He wants us to follow boldly, bravely, and proudly. We can be confident that those who trust in Him will never be ashamed.

The Lord is good,
a refuge in times of trouble.
He cares for those
who trust in him.

NAHUM 1:7 NIV

Today there is a Warrior protecting you,
a Shepherd leading you,
a Counselor instructing you,
a High Priest representing you,
a Comforter encouraging you,
a Father loving you!

*My soul yearns
for you in the night;
in the morning
my spirit longs for you.*

ISAIAH 26:9 NIV

The troubled surface of a lake will not reflect an object clearly. Wind blowing over the land will keep the dew from settling on the grass. Even so, the image of God is seen the clearest when we are at rest in Him, and the refreshing of His Spirit settles on us when we quiet our souls before Him.

*How priceless
is your unfailing love!
Both high and low
among men find refuge
in the shadow
of your wings.*

PSALM 36:7 NIV

The Lord wants us to
look upon His face,
gaze upon His beauty,
lean upon His breast,
rest within His arms,
abide under His shadow,
hide beneath His wings,
delight within His love!

*For the Lord God
is a sun and shield:
the Lord will give
grace and glory;
no good thing
will he withhold
from them
that walk uprightly.*

PSALM 84:11

*B*ecause God is your
Father you shall not

WANT,
Psalm 23:1

PERISH,
John 3:16

BE IN BONDAGE TO SIN,
Romans 6:14

FIGHT YOUR OWN BATTLES,
2 Chronicles 20:17

WITHER,
Psalm 1:3

BE FORGOTTEN,
Psalm 9:18

BE MOVED.
Psalm 16:8

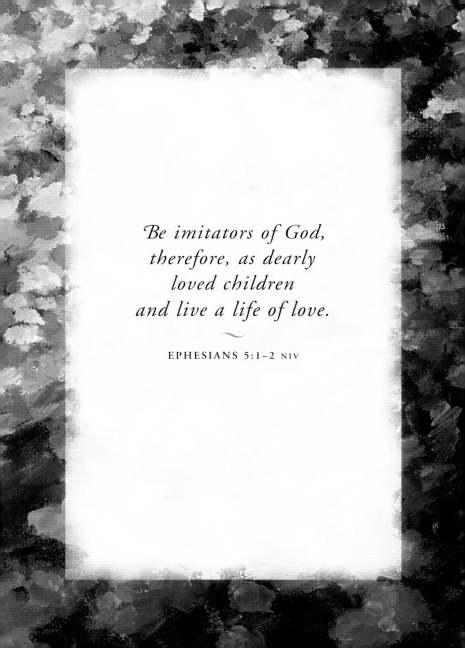

Be imitators of God,
therefore, as dearly
loved children
and live a life of love.

~

EPHESIANS 5:1–2 NIV

hat can compare to being God's child? It is a happier, hardier, healthier, and holier life than any other.

And I will restore to you the years that the locust hath eaten, the cankerworm, and the caterpiller, and the palmerworm, my great army which I sent among you. And ye shall eat in plenty, and be satisfied, and praise the name of the Lord your God, that hath dealt wondrously with you.

JOEL 2:25–26

God's purpose is not to destroy us,
but to restore us.
The enemy is the destroyer,
but God has promised to restore
the things the enemy has taken from our lives.
All the years of lost joy,
all the times of frustration and defeat,
all the moments of regret,
all the pains of lost opportunities,
all the hurts of broken relationships
God will restore to you.
He is building His kingdom within you—
a kingdom of joy, love, peace, righteousness,
victory, redemption, and right relationships.

*When my spirit grows
faint within me,
it is you who know my way....
I cry to you, O Lord;
I say, "You are my refuge,
my portion in the land
of the living."*

~

PSALM 142:3,5 NIV

*H*e is the God of the multitude and the God of the individual. He is the God of the highways in our lives and also the God of the byways. He is the God of the big things that concern us and the little things. He does mighty works and sees to the smallest detail. Nothing you face is too big for Him to handle, and He will not overlook your tiniest need.

*He who did not
spare his own Son,
but gave him up
for us all—how
will he not also,
along with him,
graciously give us
all things?*

ROMANS 8:32 NIV

*B*ecause God is your
Father you shall not

SLIDE,
Psalm 26:1

FEAR,
Psalm 27:3

WANT ANY GOOD THING,
Psalm 34:10

BE ASHAMED,
Psalm 37:19

LACK,
Proverbs 28:27

STUMBLE,
Proverbs 3:23

MAKE HASTE.
Isaiah 28:16

Oh how great is thy goodness,
which thou hast laid up
for them that fear thee;
which thou hast wrought
for them that trust in thee
before the sons of men!...
Blessed be the Lord:
for he hath shewed me
his marvellous kindness.

PSALM 31:19,21

*H*e is not the God of the "half-empty" or "half-full" in our lives. He is the God of the "exceeding abundantly above all we could ask or think." His will for us is not just joy but great joy; not just peace, but the peace that passes understanding; not just love, but fullness of love; not just to be a conqueror, but to be more than a conqueror. When He fills our cup, it is overflowing. When He flows through us, it is as rivers of living water. When He meets a need, He does it out of the riches that are in Christ.

*To whom God would
make known what is
the riches of the glory
of this mystery
among the Gentiles;
which is Christ in you,
the hope of glory.*

COLOSSIANS 1:27

You are victorious today because Christ is in you.
You are not separated from Him.
You don't have to go anyplace to find Him;
you don't have to do anything to earn Him.
The treasure is within.
There is no need to ask God
for something you already have.
The issue today is not your weakness,
but His strength; not your efforts,
but His life; not your inadequacies,
but His sufficiency.
You are Christ's and your life
is hidden with Him in God.

ROY LESSIN

*In my distress I called
to the Lord,
and he answered me.*

~

JONAH 2:2 NIV

*Incline your ear,
and come unto me:
hear, and your soul
shall live.*

~

ISAIAH 55:3

When God speaks to you, He will not say things like: "What's the use?" or "You are hopeless!" or "Can't you do anything right?" or "You will never amount to anything!" His voice is the sound of a loving Heavenly Father. He is your best friend and closest companion. You are His joint-heir in Christ, the bride of His beloved Son. His voice is the best sound you can hear.

*O the depth of the riches
both of the wisdom and knowledge
of God! How unsearchable
are his judgments,
and his ways past finding out!*

~

ROMANS 11:33

All of God's children know His discipline. He disciplines us to correct us, not to judge us; to assure us, not to condemn us; to affirm us, not to reject us. His correcting hand is clothed in lovingkindness. All He does is in faithfulness. All He desires is in goodness. All He wills is in kindness. We are much better off to have Him discipline us than to ignore us. His correction reveals how much He values us.

*"Are not two sparrows sold
for a farthing? And one of them
shall not fall on the ground
without your Father. But
the very hairs of your head
are all numbered.
Fear ye not therefore,
ye are of more value
than many sparrows."*

MATTHEW 10:29–31

There is no place beyond His strength,
no boundaries to His love,
no limit to His mercies,
no problem outside His solution,
no need beyond His care.

Do not fear...
The Lord your God
is with you...
He will quiet you
with his love.

~

ZEPHANIAH 3:16–17 NIV

*S*ometimes the Lord
calms the storm;
sometimes He lets the storm rage
and calms His child.

Be still,
and know
that I am God.

~

PSALM 46:10

I am so busy, Lord;
there is so much to do.
Can all of these busy
things be from You?

Delete your agenda;
let your soul be still.
There's always time
enough to do My will!

*The Lord is faithful
to all his promises
and loving toward
all he has made.*

PSALM 145:13 NIV

*L*ive in the relaxation of knowing that God has accepted you. Live in the confidence of knowing that Christ's blood makes you worthy. Live in the assurance that He is holding your hand. Live in the joy of knowing you are forgiven.

We love because he first loved us.

1 JOHN 4:19 NIV

But when the kindness and love of God our Savior appeared, he saved us not because of righteous things we had done, but because of his mercy. He saved us through the washing of rebirth and renewal by the Holy Spirit.

TITUS 3:4–5 NIV

The Lord fills your heart with great joy,
your soul with great delight,
your life with the beauty of His glory.
He makes you glad in His love,
rich in His grace,
whole in His mercy and His kindness.

ROY LESSIN

The Lord is gracious,
and full of compassion;
slow to anger,
and of great mercy.
The Lord is good to all;
and his tender mercies
are over all his works.

~

PSALM 145:8–9

The Lord stretches out His arms toward
you so you can see how strong they are.
He shows you His hands so you can
know how caring they are. He reveals
His ways so you can know how good
they are. He shares His desires so
you can know how loving they are.

*Remember ye not the former things,
neither consider the things of old.
Behold, I will do a new thing; now it
shall spring forth; shall ye not know it?
I will even make a way in the wilderness,
and rivers in the desert.*

ISAIAH 43:18–19

*W*hen God takes our lives,
He turns a wasteland into a forest.
He puts within us

THE CEDAR
(a tree associated with worship),

THE ACACIA
(associated with service),

THE MYRTLE
(associated with fragrance),

THE OLIVE
(associated with anointing),

THE PINE
(associated with consistency),

THE FIR
(associated with praise),

AND THE CYPRESS
(associated with fruitfulness).

"I am the light of the world.
Whoever follows me
will never walk in darkness,
but will have the light of life."

~

JOHN 8:12 NIV

*I*n your walk with God, you are always moving on—from faith to faith, from glory to glory. Your knowledge of Him will increase; your love for Him will grow; your hope in Him will become stronger. The fragrance of your life will become sweeter, and your light will shine brighter until that perfect day.

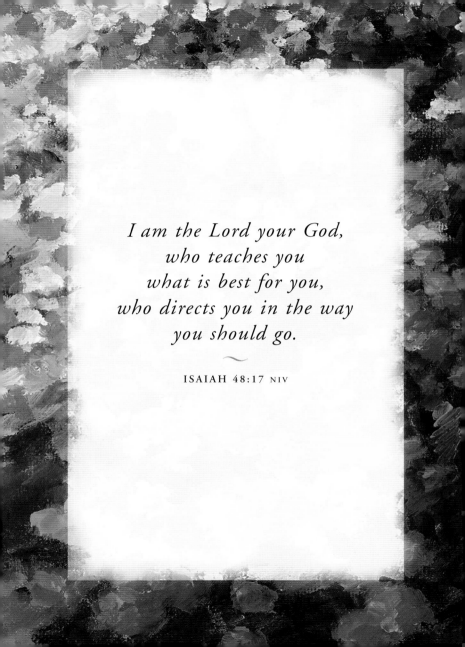

*I am the Lord your God,
who teaches you
what is best for you,
who directs you in the way
you should go.*

⌒

ISAIAH 48:17 NIV

God wants us to live with His "yes" upon our
lives. The greatest things come from Him,
are through Him, and go back to Him. There
is nothing more important than to have His
approval or consent, His blessing upon our
thoughts and our actions. Our hearts should
seek to make His heart glad. The greatest
words a son can hear from his father are,
"This is my son in whom I am well pleased."

The Lord is my shepherd;
I shall not want.

PSALM 23:1

As your shepherd the Lord is
    Always watching,
    Always keeping,
    Always providing,
    Always defending,
    Never forsaking.

*And the Lord
direct your hearts
into the love of God,
and into the patient
waiting for Christ.*

2 THESSALONIANS 3:5

The Christian life is Christ's life in you. It is not a creed, a theory, a principle, a ritual, or a religion. You are the receiver of this life. He is the origin, the producer, and the sustainer of this life. His life is a reality. He does not give a fake life or a substitute. You are alive because Christ lives in you. He is more than your helper or comforter—He is your life! He is all there is and all that really matters.

ROY LESSIN IS A COFOUNDER OF DAYSPRING CARDS, THE
PREMIER CHRISTIAN CARD COMPANY. HE IS THE AUTHOR
OF MORE THAN A DOZEN BOOKS, INCLUDING *FORGIVEN*,
WHICH WAS A FINALIST FOR A GOLD MEDALLION AWARD
FOR BEST INSPIRATIONAL BOOK. LESSIN IS A GRADUATE
OF BETHANY COLLEGE OF MISSIONS AND HAS BEEN
ACTIVE IN MISSION WORK, CHRISTIAN EDUCATION, AND
COUNSELING.

Additional copies of this book
are available from your local bookstore.

Also by Roy Lessin:
From God's Heart to Yours

If you have enjoyed this book, or if it has
impacted your life, we would like to hear from you.

Please contact us at:
**Honor Books
Department E
P.O. Box 55388
Tulsa, Oklahoma 74155**

Or by e-mail at info@honorbooks.com